Do you know any grown-ups?

Of course you do. They're everywhere. You can't walk down the street without seeing one. And, mostly, they do a very good job. They look after us, they drive us around in cars and they cook us nice food. Sometimes, they even buy us presents and treats.

Grown-ups are all right.

Generally speaking.

But my grown-up is a bit different. He's my uncle and he's . . . well, you'll find out.

His name is Foulpest, which is strange enough, but the things he gets up to are so totally and completely weird and nutty that just thinking about them makes me go all red and wobbly.

So when I tell my stories, I like to pretend they all happened to someone else.

Don't get me wrong. I love my uncle. He has a good heart and he tries very hard, but he's just . . .

Well, he's just my uncle Foulpest.

Wally

DINOSAUR DISASTER

Wally woke up.

'Oh dear,' he thought.

He didn't feel at all well. His throat was dry. His head throbbed. His whole body ached. There was no way he was going to be able to go to school today. Wally loved school. School made him feel normal and, with an ogre for an uncle, normal was important. So Wally couldn't bear the idea of missing a day.

Wait a minute, though. What was he thinking? Today was Saturday!

So that was okay. He'd just have a nice cup of tea and stay in bed. He was sure to feel better by Monday.

Then he remembered.

If today was Saturday, that meant Tommy's party was this lunchtime!

Wally had been looking forward to the party for weeks. Everyone would be there - including Sam, Wally's best friend.

Tommy was a girl - her real name was Thomasina - and one of the reasons Wally liked being her friend was that she always had brilliant parties. Last year, she'd had a pirate party and there'd been peg-leg races and sword-fighting and an actual plank you could walk - into a big tub of goo!

The year before, she'd had a space party and everyone had come as aliens and Tommy's mum and dad had decorated their whole garden so that it looked like a different planet: there were purple plants, and giant toadstools you could sit on, and the shed was painted to look like a crashed rocket ship.

And this year would be best of all, because this year Tommy's party was going to be a... a...

Hmm.

Wally couldn't remember!

'Blimey!' he thought. 'I *must* be ill.'

But whatever kind of party it was, it was bound to be wonderful.

And he was going to miss it!

Maybe he *wasn't* as ill as all that...

Maybe he was just feeling a bit peaky. He might still get better in time for the party.

Wally staggered into the bathroom to get a look at himself in the mirror.

Oh no.

His face and body were covered in little blisters that itched like crazy.

There was no doubt about it. He had chicken-pox.

'Oh, rats!' Wally cried.

'What's the matter, boy?' asked his uncle Foulpest as he came into the bathroom. Foulpest was an ogre – a real one, with warts and great big pointy ears with hairs sticking out of them and everything.

'Just look at me!' said Wally.

'Ooh, yes,' said Foulpest. 'Those blisters! All disgusting and crusty and bulging with gunge. I know just the thing. Don't move.'

'What are you going to get?' said Wally. 'Some medicine?'

'No, my camera,' said Foulpest.

'I haven't seen boils this brilliant for months! *Scab* magazine would pay a fortune for a picture of them.'

Ogres love great big scabby blisters.

'You are NOT sending a picture of my blisters to *Scab* magazine!' said Wally.

'How about *Spot Weekly*?' said Foulpest.

'No,' said Wally.

'*Beautiful Boils*?' said Foulpest.

'No,' said Wally.

'*Junior Pimple Burster*?' said Foulpest.

'No, no, no!' said Wally.

'I'll share the money with you,' said Foulpest.

'I don't want money,' said Wally, 'I just want to go to Tommy's party.'

'Is that today?' said Foulpest. 'What kind of party is she having this year?'

'I don't know!' said Wally. 'I can't remember!'

'Blimey!' said Foulpest. 'You must be ill. That's a shame. Course, when I were a lad, I dreamed of being covered in blisters. Every year, me school gave a prize to the young ogre who'd grown the most disgusting boils. Me Gran even cooked me up a chicken-pox mixture so I'd get extra ones. Oh, I was a right perishing sight after I drunk that, I can tell you!'

'Did you win the prize?' asked Wally.

'No,' said Foulpest bitterly. 'I got beat by Scroffcheeks in me class. Lucky devil got some really horrible disease the day before the award was given out. It turned his whole head into one ginormous pimple! It was not blooming fair!'

Suddenly, Wally felt even more unwell.

'You're not looking too good, Wally boy,' said Foulpest. 'You need to get tucked up in bed this minute. Rest, that's what you want, and plenty of it.'

Wally flopped down on his bed, feeling exhausted, but it was very difficult to get to sleep. For a start, he was far too hot. As he tossed and turned, trying to get comfortable, he kept thinking about his friends and all the fun they'd be having at the party this lunchtime.

It wasn't fair!

But there was nothing he could do about it.

At long last, his eyes started to close . . .

Then Foulpest burst into the room.

'Wally boy!' Foulpest cried. 'Don't go to sleep, I've had a perishing idea! You *will* go to that party, after all!'

'Why are we standing out here by the back door, Uncle Foulpest?' asked Wally.

'Because this is where the bins are, silly,' said Foulpest.

'And what are you doing in the bins?' asked Wally.

'I'm going through them, aren't I?' said Foulpest, lifting his head up for a moment. There was an old tin can on his nose and thrown-away spaghetti bolognese in his hair.

'I can see that!' said Wally with a sigh. 'But why are you going through the bins?'

'Because this is where we keep the fish heads, the cheese-so-old-it's-grown-ears and the ooky gunky,' said Foulpest. 'Obviously.'

'I'm so pleased I asked,' said Wally.

'*That's* what I've been looking for!' said Foulpest, and he grabbed something disgusting from the bin, put it into a sack and went back inside.

Wally followed him into the kitchen. Foulpest was pulling lots of disgusting things out of his sack and throwing them into the cooking bucket where they sizzled and blerched.

'For the last time,' said Wally, '*what* is going on?'

'You remember how I said that my Gran cooked me up a chicken-pox mixture so I'd grow extra boils?' said Foulpest.

'Yes,' said Wally grimly. He'd been doing his best to forget everything Foulpest had told him about his school's prize for disgusting boils.

'Well, it turns out I've got the recipe with me!' said Foulpest. He pulled a torn bit of rag out of his pocket. 'That's a stroke of perishing luck, isn't it?'

'Is it?' said Wally. 'What good is that going to do me? I want to get *rid* of my blisters, not grow extra ones.'

'That's just the blooming point,' said Foulpest, 'because I'm going to cook the recipe backwards. If I do that, the mixture is bound to work backwards.

16

It won't *give* you blisters, it will take them away! It stands to reason, don't it?'

'Does it?' said Wally, who wasn't at all sure. 'Ooh, my goodness! What's that awful pong?'

'That's the mixture,' said Foulpest, pointing to the stinky ooze bubbling in his cooking bucket. 'Oh, fill your hooter with it!' Foulpest took a big sniff. 'That's the smell of my Gran's cooking. Nothing in the world quite like it.'

'It smells like armpits,' said Wally.

'It's got armpits in it,' said Foulpest.

Wally grabbed the torn bit of rag and looked at the recipe.

1 handful of
fish heads, rotten

1 ear of
cheese-so-old-it's-grown-ears

3 cups of ooky gunk

2 ripe armpits

8 teaspoons
of verruca juice

A sprinkling of
dried head lice

1 roast
chicken

'One roast chicken?' said Wally.

'Of course,' said Foulpest. 'It's for chicken-pox, isn't it? You should see the one for German measles. You have to add an actual German. They put up quite a fight.'

'I think the sock's just there to make it look nice,' said Foulpest.

'I think I'm going to be ill,' said Wally.

'You *are* ill,' said Foulpest. 'The question is: do you want to get better?'

Wally thought of Tommy's party. He thought of all the wonderful fun he could have there, doing . . .

Doing *what* exactly?

He still couldn't remember what kind of party it was going to be!

He so wanted to go. But he wasn't at all sure about Foulpest's backwards mixture. He needed to think long and hard about what to do.

Which was a shame, because while Wally was busy thinking, Foulpest pinched his nose and poured a cupful of the horrible mixture straight down his throat.

'Fleurk!' Wally spluttered. 'Neurk! Bleurk!'

'Delicious, isn't it?' said Foulpest. 'My Gran's a brilliant cook. You should try her Sneeze on Toast. I can see it now, all green and crispy and bubbling. And the things she could do with scabs! Scab puffs, scab salad sandwiches. . . Yum!'

Foulpest licked his lips, but Wally wasn't listening. He was far too busy feeling peculiar.

His skin tingled. His blisters twitched. He felt a huge hot bezoinging in his bottom.

'Yeuch!' he cried. 'What did you do that for, uncle? Pouring funny mixtures into people is very dangerous! Who knows what it's done to me? My skin tingled, my blisters twitched and I felt a huge hot bezoinging in my. . . '

Wally stopped speaking. He'd just caught sight of himself in the mirror.

'I don't believe it!' he said. He looked closer. 'Foulpest! Look at me! My blisters have vanished.'

'Erm, yeah,' said Foulpest.

'Never mind "Erm, yeah",' said Wally. He grabbed Foulpest and kissed him. 'You're a marvel! And so is your Gran!'

'Hmmm,' Foulpest mumbled.

'What's the matter?' said Wally. 'I thought you'd be pleased. It worked! I'm going to the party after all!'

'You might want to take a closer look. . . ' said Foulpest.

'What are you talking about?' said Wally.

'I'm cured. My chicken-pox has gone. My head doesn't throb any more. My body doesn't ache. My tail feels fantastic . . . Hang on a minute.'

'I think I'll just pop out for a walk,' said Foulpest.

'You're going nowhere!' said Wally. 'I've got a *tail!*'

'Yes,' said Foulpest. 'I had noticed that. Shame.'

'And not just any tail!' said Wally. 'It's a great big dinosaur tail! So *that's* what that huge hot bezoinging in my bottom was! I was growing a tail – and a pair of dinosaur legs to go with it! But how did that happen?'

Foulpest poked around inside his cooking bucket.

'That's how,' he said. He reached in and brought out a scrap of wrapping paper with dinosaurs on it. 'It must have been stuck to the ooky gunk. Or the cheese-so-old-it's-grown-ears. That's the problem with cooking things out of the bin. You can't be sure they're completely clean.'

Ding dong!

It was the doorbell.

'You've got to answer it, Uncle Foulpest,' said Wally. 'I can't go to the door like this.'

'Answer what?' said Foulpest. He was still poking around, deep inside the cooking bucket, and hadn't heard the bell.

Ding dong! Ding dong!

'Oh dear!' said Wally as he waddled to

the front door.

He looked through the spyhole: it was his best friend, Sam.

What was he going to do?

Wally opened the door just a fraction so Sam wouldn't see his dinosaur legs and tail, and popped his head out.

'Hello, Wally,' said Sam. 'I was wondering if you wanted to come round to play at my house this morning. Then we could go to Tommy's party together.'

'Erm. . . ' said Wally. 'No, sorry.'

'Is there something wrong?' asked Sam.

'No!' said Wally. 'I mean, yes! I mean, I'm ill.'

'Are you sure?' said Sam. 'You don't *look* ill.'

'I'm only a bit ill,' said Wally. 'That is, only a bit of me is ill.'

'What bit?' asked Sam.

'My bottom,' Wally said – and immediately wished he hadn't.

'You poor thing,' said Sam. 'I hope you get better by lunchtime."

'Me too. Bye!' said Wally, and he closed the door quickly.

Wally's head was spinning. He felt himself start to fall over. He was going to land face down on the floor. But at the last minute, his dinosaur tail caught him.

'Thank you,' said Wally. Then he realised what had happened and said, 'Wait a minute! Get off me! Yeuch! Disgusting tail! Oh, how can I go to the party now? Everyone will point at me and laugh!'

'I know just what to do,' said Foulpest, who was standing in the hall behind him. 'Don't move.'

'You are *not* going to take a picture of me and sell it to *Nephews With Tails* magazine!' said Wally.

'But you'll be famous!' said Foulpest.

'I don't *want* to be famous!' said Wally. 'Not for having a horrible dinosaur tail anyway!'

'They'll pay us pots of cash!' said Foulpest.

'No,' said Wally firmly.

'All right,' said Foulpest. 'Let me think.' Then he clapped his hand to his forehead. 'I know what!' he cried. 'I'll make some more chicken-pox mixture! Only this time I'll make it the *right* way round. If making the mixture backwards has given you a tail, making it the right way round should take the tail away again, shouldn't it?'

'But what if it doesn't?' said Wally. 'What if it all goes horribly wrong? I could end up with a tail *and* chicken-pox!'

Foulpest's eyes flashed with joy.

'That would be *amazing!*' he said. 'I'll get cooking right now!'

'No you will not,' said Wally firmly. 'You will take me to the doctor.'

'But—' said Foulpest.

'Please,' said Wally.

'Oh, all right,' said Foulpest. 'What a thumping waste!'

When they got to the doctor's, Wally recognised some of the people in the waiting room.

'Oh no!' he cried and he stepped back out into the corridor.

'Where are you going, Wally?' said Foulpest. 'You were the one who wanted to come here.'

'You see those people sitting over there?' said Wally.

He pointed through the glass door.

'Where?' said Foulpest, pressing his face up against the glass so hard it cracked.

'Don't look, they'll see you!' said Wally.

'But you've just perishing told me to look!' said Foulpest.

'Never mind that,' said Wally. 'It's Bernard from my class, and his mum and dad.'

'You mean that big grey lady?' said Foulpest. 'Who looks like a thwacking great battleship in shoes? And the very short round man, who looks like a football in a suit?'

'That's right,' said Wally. 'Bernard's the one sitting in between them. He's always eating and cheating and saying horrible things. If he sees me with this tail, he'll tell everyone. I'll be a laughing stock!'

'But he's not going to see you, is he? Poor little chap,' chuckled Foulpest. 'He's got a dirty great biscuit tin stuck on his head! Come on, let's go and see if we can help.'

'Foulpest, no!' cried Wally, but it was too late.

Foulpest walked into the waiting room and right up to Bernard and his mum and dad.

Wally did his best to stuff his dinosaur tail down the back of his trousers, where no one would see it, and waddled in after him.

But before Wally had a chance to pull him away, Foulpest had smiled at Bernard's mum and dad and said, 'Hello there.'

Bernard's mum and dad looked him up and down with a sneer.

'Good moaning,' said Bernard's mum coldly.

'Foulpest's the name,' said Foulpest, and he held out his hand.

Bernard's mum and dad stared at it like it was grot from underneath their toenails, but Foulpest didn't seem to mind.

'It looks like your boy needs some help,' he said.

'He's quite all right, thank you,' said Bernard's mum.

'I am not!' said Bernard from inside the biscuit tin. 'This is boring and rubbish! I'm hungry! Why haven't you got this tin off my head yet? You're boring and rubbish!'

'Don't you worry your little heart

about it, my lovely darling,' said Bernard's mum. 'Mummy and Daddy have brought you to the doctor's. She'll get that nasty old biscuit tin off your head in no time.'

'Then what are we waiting for?' said Bernard. 'Tell her to do it now!'

'We have to take our turn, old boy,' said Bernard's dad in a squeaky voice. 'It's only fair.'

'Shut up!' said Bernard's mum. 'How dare you talk to my darling boy like that?'

'Sorry, dear,' squeaked Bernard's dad.

'I hate you both!' said Bernard. 'You smell!'

'The poor little mite's in a bit of a state,' said Bernard's mum. 'It happened this morning,' she explained. 'He'd just had his breakfast and he was feeling peckish. . .'

'I was starving hungry, woman!' said Bernard. 'You'd only given me eight sausages, six eggs, two packets of bacon, half a loaf of toast and some sweets. You are so mean!'

'So I said to him, "Why don't you have a little biscuit, darling?"' said Bernard's mum. 'And I opened him up a brand new tin of biscuits. Well, I could see he was hungry by the way he plunged his lovely little head right into it.'

'But when he tried to get his lovely little head out of it again, it was stuck, is that right?' said Foulpest.

'If you ask me, they make these biscuit tins far too small,' said Bernard's mum. 'I've a good mind to write to the newspapers about it.'

'Never mind all that rubbish,' said Bernard, 'just get this rotten thing off my head! I've eaten all the biscuits in here and now I'm starving again and I've got a party to go to.'

'Is he going to Tommy's party too?' said Foulpest. 'My nephew Wally's going to that, once we've sorted out the problem with his bottom. Aren't you, Wally?'

'Wally's got a problem with his bottom?' said Bernard.

Wally just wanted to disappear.

'Will one of you idiots get this biscuit tin off my head immediately?' said Bernard. 'I want to see what's wrong with Wally's bottom!'

'Oh, bless,' said Foulpest. 'He really cares about his friend, doesn't he? Well, we can't have you missing the party, can we? Come here, lad.'

And before Wally could stop him, Foulpest had grabbed hold of the biscuit tin on Bernard's head and was trying to pull it off.

'What are you *doing?*' cried Bernard's mum.

'Won't take a second,' said Foulpest. He started twisting the biscuit tin. 'I bet it's just like getting the top off the ketchup bottle.'

'Help!' shrieked Bernard.

'Crikey, it's harder than it looks,' said Foulpest. 'I'll have to put a bit more elbow grease into this. *Gnnnnnrrrrr!*'

'Let go of him at once!' cried Bernard's mum.

'I need some purchase,' said Foulpest. He trod on Bernard's feet and yanked the biscuit tin upwards.

'Argh!' screamed Bernard.

'Don't just stand there, Geoffrey,' said Bernard's mum to Bernard's dad. 'Do something!'

'Certainly, dear,' squeaked Bernard's dad. He rolled up a magazine and began hitting Foulpest with it, crying 'Unhand him, you brute!'

But Foulpest was so large, and was concentrating so hard on the biscuit tin, that he didn't even notice.

'So what sort of party is it, then?' he asked Bernard. 'Only Wally can't remember.'

'Police! Police!' cried Bernard's mum.

'A police party, eh?' said Foulpest. 'That sounds like fun. Now, what I really need to do is jam you in the door, young man. . . All it would take then is a really good pull and - woomph - it'll come clean off.' Foulpest stuck Bernard under his arm and marched towards the door.

'Oh my goodness!' screamed Bernard's mum. 'He's going to pull my lovely darling's head off! Well come on, you lot, help us!'

The rest of the people in the waiting room - who had runny noses, or spotty faces, or legs in plaster - had been hiding behind their newspapers, trying to pretend the whole terrible thing wasn't happening. But now Bernard's mum was shouting at them and hitting them with her handbag and they couldn't avoid it any more.

Some grabbed hold of Foulpest and some grabbed hold of Bernard and they tried to pull the two of them apart.

'Isn't this brilliant?' Foulpest smiled at Wally. 'Everyone's pitching in to help. Here we go, folks! One, two, three!'

Foulpest pulled so hard that the people hanging onto Bernard were jerked forward. They all let go at once and went flying.

Foulpest himself was sent spinning backwards across the room. He was waving Bernard around so fast that he knocked everyone else over.

But still the biscuit tin wouldn't come off.

'We nearly did it that time,' said Foulpest. He knocked on the biscuit tin.

'How are you feeling in there, lad?'

'Eeeurgh,' said Bernard from inside, and his body went limp.

'You've killed him!' cried Bernard's mum, and she fainted.

'Nurse! Nurse!' squeaked Bernard's dad.

'I wish I could run him under the hot tap,' said Foulpest. 'Unless anyone's got any butter?'

'Just let go of him, Foulpest!' cried Wally.

'I've definitely loosened it,' said Foulpest.

He was now shaking the biscuit tin very hard. Bernard's arms and legs were flapping wildly around like the tentacles of a floppy octopus.

'That's it!' cried Foulpest suddenly. 'Get ready because here... he... comes...!'

With a sucking slurping noise, Bernard's

head finally came sliding out of the tin and Bernard went shooting across the waiting room...

... straight towards a large window.

'Stop him, he'll be cut to ribbons!' squeaked Bernard's dad.

But just as Bernard was about to smash into the window, Wally caught him.

With his tail.

'Nice catch, Wally boy,' said Foulpest proudly.

'But. . . But. . . ' stammered Bernard's dad, pointing at Wally's tail, and he fainted too.

At that moment, the receptionist walked in.

'The doctor will see you now,' she said.

'About time too!' said Bernard. 'My head hurts!'

It didn't take long for the doctor to check Bernard over, and send him home with an ice pack for his sore head.

Then she called Wally and Foulpest in, and spent a long time staring at Wally's tail.

She poked it and prodded it, and walked around it and got underneath it to see what it looked like from down there.

'Mmm,' she said thoughtfully, and 'Yes,' and 'Well I never!'

At last she stopped, and nodded her head wisely.

'Well, doctor,' said Wally, 'what can we do?'

'Now that I've given you a thorough examination,' said the doctor, 'I think there's only one thing we can do.'

'What's that?' said Foulpest.

'Cut a hole in your trousers,' said the doctor.

'What?' said Wally.

'At the back there,' said the doctor.
'So your tail has a bit more room to swish
about.'

'Swish about?' said Wally.

'Well, you don't want it getting cramp,
do you?'

'Cramp?' said Wally. 'I don't care
about it getting cramp! It's a tail! And
it's sticking out of my bottom! So would

you please get rid of it? By lunchtime if possible. I am going to a party.'

'Get rid of it?' said the doctor. 'What do you want to do a silly thing like that for? You should enjoy it! Oh, I've always wanted a tail. If I had a tail, I wouldn't need my bicycle. I could just swing down the street from one lamppost to the next.'

'It's not a monkey tail,' said Wally grumpily. 'It's a dinosaur tail.'

'And think of the money we could earn from *Nephews With Tails* magazine,' said Foulpest.

'Never mind *Nephews With Tails* magazine!' snapped Wally.

'Or I could coil my tail up like a spring and boingy-oing to work in the morning,' said the doctor.

'It's not a kangaroo tail either,' said Wally. 'Have you all gone stark staring bonkers? I have to get rid of this tail and the sooner the better. I need you to tell me how!'

The doctor looked disappointed.

'Well, if you're really sure. . . ' she said.

'Of course I'm sure!' said Wally.

'I suppose you could try wart remover cream,' the doctor said. 'But you'd need an awful lot to shift something that big.'

'You've got wart REMOVER cream?' said Foulpest, horrified.

He was particularly proud of his warts. He would never dream of removing them.

'If I used cream,' said Wally, 'would my tail be gone by lunchtime?'

'No chance,' said the doctor. 'If only you'd come in with chicken-pox.

We've got this amazing new pill which clears up chicken-pox in ten minutes flat.'

The moment they got back home, Foulpest started making a new mixture.

'And you're sure this one is going to give me chicken-pox?' said Wally.

'Yes, because this time I'm making it the right way round,' said Foulpest. 'Like my Gran did when she wanted to give me chicken-pox. You should have seen the blisters that popped out on my face! Big and green and bursting with gunge, they were!'

Foulpest smiled happily and gave Wally a cupful of the mixture.

'I can't believe I'm doing this,' said Wally.

'Drink up,' said Foulpest. 'While there's still time.'

Wally looked at the clock. It was a quarter to twelve. Tommy's party started at half past.

'I'll drink the new potion,' said Wally.

'I'll go back to having chicken-pox. We'll go back to the doctor. She'll give me this amazing new pill. I'll get better and still be in time for the party. Just.'

'Unless, of course,' said Foulpest, 'this mixture makes things even worse.'

'Worse?' said Wally. 'How could things possibly get any worse?'

He held his nose and drank the mixture.

'Oh dear,' said Foulpest.

'Now what?' said Wally.

'Well. . . ' said Foulpest.

'Have I still got my tail?' said Wally.

'Oh yeah,' said Foulpest.

'So that revolting potion did nothing at all?' cried Wally.

'I wouldn't say that,' Foulpest replied.

'But my skin feels funny,' said Wally. 'All crinkly and crusty. I must have got my chicken-pox back.'

'Have a look in the mirror,' said Foulpest.

Wally did.

'Argh!' he screamed. His voice came out sounding funny too.

It was no wonder. He still had his dinosaur tail and legs. But now he also had a dinosaur head and a dinosaur body to go with it!

'There must have been more dinosaur wrapping paper in the mixture than I thought,' said Foulpest.

Wally looked at the clock.

'Oh well, that's it then,' he said sadly. 'There's no way I'm going to the party now.'

His eyes felt hot. He was going to cry.

'Oh, hey, don't do that!' said Foulpest. 'It's all right, lad! Come here.'

Foulpest reached out to give Wally a big hug, but he kept getting poked by Wally's spikes and plates and horns.

'Ooh! Ahh! Ouch!' Foulpest cried.

In the end he gave up and just patted Wally on his scaly back.

'Oh, Uncle Foulpest!' cried Wally in despair. 'What am I going to do?'

'Don't worry, lad,' said Foulpest. 'It's bound to wear off sooner or later.'

'But the party will be over by then!' cried Wally miserably.

'There'll be plenty more perishing parties,' said Foulpest.

'Not like this one. This is one of TOMMY'S parties!' said Wally.

'And in the meantime,' said Foulpest, 'think of all the things you can do now you're a dinosaur.'

'Such as?' said Wally.

'Erm,' said Foulpest. 'You can scratch the back of your ear with your tail.'

'Oh fabulous!' said Wally. 'That's worth missing a party for, isn't it? Is there no way you can turn me back into me in time?'

'Well, there was one thing my Gran used to give us when her mixtures went all wrong,' said Foulpest. 'That usually put us back to normal.'

'And what was it?' said Wally.

'It's funny you should ask, Wally lad,' said Foulpest. 'I can't remember.'

'Oh for goodness sake!' bellowed Wally in his new dinosaur voice.

'Calm down, lad,' said Foulpest. 'Have a bun.'

'But I don't eat buns!' Wally yelled. 'I'm a dinosaur now! I only eat plants! You couldn't even make me an exciting, meat-eating dinosaur. At least then I could have had some fun. I could have gone crashing up and down the road eating shops and scaring the postman. But oh no, I had to be one of the boring ones that just sit around all day, chewing moss and scratching the backs of their ears!' And he roared a dinosaur roar, 'Grrrarrrll!' and went rampaging around the house. He knocked over furniture and his stamping feet sent cracks splintering across the floor and up the walls.

'That looked like fun,' said Foulpest when Wally had finished.

'But I'm still a dinosaur,' said Wally.

'Hey!' said Foulpest excitedly. 'You know that thing that Gran used to give us when her mixtures went all wrong?'

'Yes?' said Wally hopefully.

'I still can't remember what it is,' said Foulpest.

'Oh, I'm going to see Mrs Beamish,' said Wally.

Mrs Beamish was the nice old lady from next door. Wally always went to see her with his problems because she was friendly, kind and helpful, and baked really wonderful fairy cakes.

'Hello, Wally,' she said when she opened the door. 'Been turned into a dinosaur, have you?'

Mrs Beamish had lived next to Foulpest and Wally for such a long time that she wasn't surprised when strange things happened to them.

'I know what,' she said, 'why don't you come in and have some fairy cakes? Then you can tell me all about it.'

'But I can only eat plants,' said Wally sadly.

'Don't worry, dear,' said Mrs Beamish. 'They'll slip down nicely with a lovely cup of tea.'

Mrs Beamish poured the tea into a large bowl and crumbled a fairy cake into it. Wally crouched forward and stretched out his long grey tongue.

The moment his tongue touched a

crumb of fairy cake floating in the bowl of tea, there was a flash! and a crash! and a shriek! And an eek! and . . .

Ding! Dong!

The doorbell rang.

'Hello, Mrs B!' said Foulpest at the door. 'Sorry to disturb you, but I've just remembered the thing that used to undo my Gran's mixtures when they went wrong! It was tea and—'

'Fairy cakes,' said Wally in his own voice.

'Look at you, lad!' said Foulpest. 'You're not a dinosaur any more, you're back to being a boy! Oh, thank you, Mrs Beamish. That was wonderful!'

Foulpest grabbed Mrs Beamish and gave her a big hug.

'That's all right, dear. It was only some tea and fairy cake,' said Mrs Beamish. 'Now please let go of me. I'm going purple.'

'Oh yes, of course, sorry,' said Foulpest. 'Don't know me own perishing strength sometimes!'

'And look at the time,' said Wally.

'Twenty past twelve!' said Foulpest. 'There's still time for you to get to the party.'

'Just,' said Wally. 'Thank you for everything, Mrs Beamish, but I have to go.'

He kissed her, hugged Foulpest and ran out of the house.

Wally ran so fast he was almost out of breath when he rang Tommy's doorbell.

The door was answered by a velociraptor.

'Argh!' said Wally.

'Wally,' said the velociraptor. 'We didn't think you were coming.'

'Tommy?' said Wally. 'Is that you?'

'Of course it's me!' said Tommy. 'Look, here's Sam.'

'Hi Wally,' said Sam who was dressed as a triceratops.

'Everyone's here except for you and Bernard,' said Tommy. 'Apparently, Bernard had a nasty shock at the doctor's this morning and has to stay in bed till Monday. Anyway, where's your costume?'

'My costume?' said Wally.

He looked around. There were anchylosaurs and brachiosaurs, T-Rexes and parasaurolophuses, iguanodons and spinosauruses. Everyone was dressed as a dinosaur.

Tommy's parents had decorated the whole house so that it looked like a prehistoric jungle. There were creepers and ferns, and a huge wooden volcano in the middle of the sitting room with fizzy drink bubbling in the crater.

At last Wally remembered what sort of party it was!

'Welcome to the Wild and Wonderful Dinosaur Stampede!' said a big sign hung in Tommy's living room. 'Top prize for the best dinosaur costume!'

'Grrrarrrll!' roared Wally.

At least he still sounded like a dinosaur.

HAUNTED HOUSE

Wally was in the playground one day, near the end of break-time, when he heard someone cry out, 'Help me! Please!'

Whoever it was sounded like they were in real trouble, so Wally went running off to help at once. His heart sank when he saw that it was Bernard who'd called out. Bernard was a nuisance and Wally didn't like him. He was always eating and being naughty and pouring orange drink over other people's lunches and getting bogeys absolutely everywhere.

'Wally, thank goodness you've come!' Bernard said. He was lying on the ground by the big bins. His face was white with fright and his arms and legs were stretched out as straight as they would go. 'I was just walking along, minding my own business and it. . . it. . . jumped on me!'

'What jumped on you?' asked Wally. From where he was standing, he couldn't see anything.

'It!' said Bernard with a frightened shudder. 'The spi. . . The spi. . . No, I'm too scared. I can't say it. The Ess Pee Eye Dee Ee Are.'

'The spider?' said Wally.

'Argh! Don't say that word!' shrieked Bernard. 'I'm terrified of those horrible hairy-legged beasties.'

'But spiders are just harmless little things,' said Wally. Wally didn't mind spiders, and ever since his Uncle Foulpest had moved in, Wally's house had been crawling with them. 'I'm sure it's more scared of you than you are of it.'

'I don't think so,' said Bernard. 'If I was any more scared than this, I'd go off bang.'

'Where is it?' asked Wally.

'On my t-t-tummy!' Bernard stammered. 'Ooh, I can feel it creepy-crawling along! Please can you get it off me?'

Bernard was such a nasty boy, and had been so horrible to Wally in the past, that Wally was tempted to leave him there. But he didn't want to be mean.

'Please,' said Bernard again. 'Break's nearly over and I don't want to be late for class.'

He did look very sorry for himself, so Wally said, 'Oh, all right.'

'Can you see it?' said Bernard.

'Oh yes,' said Wally, leaning towards Bernard to get a better look. 'Crumbs, it's quite a size, isn't it?'

'Don't say things like that!' snapped Bernard.

'Sorry,' said Wally.

It was a big spider, though; a lot bigger even than the big spiders

Wally sometimes found in the bath. Its eight legs were long and hairy, and its abdomen had purple and yellow stripes across it. Maybe Bernard was right to be frightened. Maybe it was a poisonous spider that had escaped from a zoo or something.

'Ah,' said Wally.

'What's the matter?' said Bernard. 'You're not chickening out, are you?'

'Nooooo,' said Wally, but he knew he didn't sound very sure.

'Just get it off me!' said Bernard. 'I think it's getting ready to pounce.'

Wally didn't like the idea of the spider pouncing on *him* either, so he crept up on it very quietly. The closer he got, the odder the spider looked. It was shiny - almost like it was made out of plastic - and those bright colours on its body didn't look real, but maybe that was the way with poisonous spiders that had escaped from the zoo.

Wally took a deep breath and reached out to brush the spider off Bernard's tummy.

And then something odd happened.

The spider turned its head to look straight at Wally - and it opened its mouth.

Wally didn't have a chance to say anything before a jet of water shot out of the spider's mouth and sprayed all over him.

'Bleurgh!' Wally cried, shutting his eyes and holding his arms up to protect himself.

'Ha! Ha! Ha!' laughed Bernard nastily and he sprang to his feet. 'Look, Wally, you great big twerp! It was only a joke spider, ha ha! A joke spider that squirts water – and you fell for it!'

'I was trying to help you,' said Wally crossly. 'You sounded like you were in trouble.'

'But I never need help!' said Bernard. 'At least, not from you!'

Wally was about to remind Bernard that, quite recently, he had needed his Uncle Foulpest's help getting his fat head out of a biscuit tin – but before he got the chance, the bell rang for the end of break.

'You'll have to hurry up and dry out, Wally,' said Bernard. 'Miss Keen won't want you in her class now you've wet yourself!'

'I haven't wet myself,' said Wally. 'You wet *me!*'

Bernard wasn't listening. He went skipping off to class, calling out, 'Wally's gone and wet himself! Wally's gone and wet himself!' in a sing-song voice loud enough for everyone to hear.

'What's Bernard on about?' said Sam, Wally's best friend, when he heard all the commotion. 'Are you all right? Has he been horrible again?'

'I've a good mind to teach him a lesson!' said Tommy – and she would have, too, if Wally hadn't stopped her.

'He's not worth it,' said Wally. 'He's just stupid. We should ignore him.'

But Wally was soaked to the skin and very cross. He tried to tell himself that it was a stupid joke. He tried to tell himself that Bernard was the one who *really* lost out from doing things like this because he didn't have any friends. He tried to tell himself that one day Bernard would be in real trouble and no one would come to help him because they'd think it was just another stupid trick.

But none of it did any good. Wally was cross and miserable – and damp – for the rest of the day.

'I'm home!' Wally called out when he got back that afternoon. He was tired and hungry and fed up, and all he wanted to do was have his drink and his biscuit and a nice sit-down in front of the television.

'Uncle Foulpest?' he called.

There was no reply.

That was odd. Usually, Foulpest came bounding up to meet him the moment he came through the door. He'd grab hold of

Wally and give him a great big hug and a kiss. Wally didn't mind a hug and a kiss – so long as no one was looking – but Uncle Foulpest was an ogre, a real one, with warts and great big pointy ears with hairs sticking out of them and everything, and his idea of a hug was to squeeze you till your bones crackled and you thought your feet were about to pop off the ends of your legs. His idea of a kiss was to blow a great big wet raspberry all over the top of your head until the spit ran down into your ears.

'Uncle Foulpest?' Wally called out again.

Again there was no reply.

Perhaps he was ill.

Wally went off to look for him.

There was no sign of Foulpest in the hall or the sitting room or the kitchen. Wally pushed open the door of the rumpus room.

'Uncle Foul—' He didn't manage to finish saying the name when his uncle reared up from behind the sofa.

'Ha! Ha!' Foulpest roared. 'Got you!'

Wally was used to Foulpest's strange behaviour, which was just as well. Anybody else who walked into a room only to have a dirty great ogre rear up at them and roar 'Got you!' would probably run shrieking into the street. Wally just said, 'There you are.'

Foulpest stood there smiling at him for a moment. Then he stopped smiling and blinked.

'Wait a minute, Wally boy,' said Foulpest. 'Why isn't you covered in brunge?'

'"Brunge"?' said Wally.

'It's short for "brown gunge",' explained Foulpest. 'It's a perishing brilliant ogre speciality. My Gran gave me the recipe years ago. You take mud gravy, rhinoceros earwax and some really big snails and you mashes them all up in a bucket—'

'Never mind that,' said Wally, interrupting, 'why did you think I was going to be covered in it?'

'Ah, well. That's the clever bit,' said Foulpest. 'You see, you takes your bucket of brunge and you opens a door, just a tiny little bit. Then you balances the bucket on top of the door. That way, the next person who opens the door all the way makes the bucket tip over and they gets covered in brunge. It's thumping hilarious!'

'Sounds it,' said Wally flatly. 'Except for one small problem. There's no bucket on top of this door.'

'Nor there isn't,' said Foulpest, standing on tiptoe to check. 'Well spotted, boy. I must have put it on another door by mistake. I wonder which one.'

And Foulpest went off upstairs to look for his bucket of brunge.

'What is the matter with everybody today?' said Wally, following him. 'Why does everyone want to play a practical joke on me?'

'I don't knows about anyone else, boy,' said Foulpest as he padded up the stairs, 'but I is doing it because I is bored.'

'Well, couldn't you think of something *nice* to do instead?' asked Wally.

'Playing practical jokes *is* nice,' said Foulpest. 'For an ogre. We only does it with the people we loves most in the whole wide world.'

Wally tried to stay fed up, but he felt a warm tickle inside when Foulpest said that.

'Think about it,' Foulpest went on,

'when you gets a bit of a scare or a spook or a fright, you feels excited, and that feels good. When you realise it's just a perishing trick, you is relieved and you laugh - and that's good too.'

'I suppose so,' said Wally - although he didn't think that was why Bernard played practical jokes.

'I bets you're a weeny bit excited now, aren't you?' said Foulpest. They were standing outside Wally's bedroom.

Wally had to admit that standing there, wondering if this was the door with the bucket of brunge balanced on it, was rather exciting.

'Okay, then, let's find out!' said Foulpest and they went barging through the door together.

Foulpest and Wally both stood there, eyes shut tight, waiting for the brunge to tip down all over them...

But nothing happened.

'No bucket up there, either,' said Wally.

'No,' said Foulpest thoughtfully. 'I wonder where I put it.'

'You know who's really good at scares and spooks and frights?' said Foulpest as they went through the house, pushing open doors, looking for the missing bucket of brunge. 'My friend Eamonn. All he has to do is blow his nose and he can give you a proper scare that'll frighten you into the middle of next week.'

'I didn't know you had a friend called

Eamonn,' said Wally.

'There's lots of things you don't know about me, Wally boy,' said Foulpest mysteriously. 'Eamonn's a Mummy.'

'A Mummy?' said Wally. 'But surely Eamonn's a boy's name.'

Foulpest laughed. 'I don't mean he's the sort of mummy who has babies! Hor hor hor!' he chortled. 'Hor hor hor!'

'It's not that funny, uncle,' said Wally.

But Foulpest couldn't stop laughing. It was clearly the funniest thing he had ever heard. He snorted so hard his nostrils flapped. 'A "Mummy"!' he spluttered. 'It's the same word as for a lady who has children! I'd never realised that before.'

'Really?' said Wally.

'Cross my heart,' said Foulpest, trying to calm down. 'Hurf hurf hurf! Just wait till I see Eamonn again. He'll laugh his bandages off when I tells him!'

'So Eamonn's the sort of Mummy who comes wrapped up in bandages, is he?' said Wally.

'That's the ticket, boy,' said Foulpest. 'Well, it makes giving people a scare or a spook or a fright a bit easier, being all wrapped up in bandages and covered in cobwebs and being thousands of years old and that. Oh, the fun we used to have! One night, he frightened me so much I actually thought I was going to be sick!'

'Really?' said Wally.

'Yeah, it was thumping marvellous!'

said Foulpest with a big smile.

Sometimes Wally thought he'd never understand his uncle.

'You'd like Eamonn,' Foulpest went on. 'I'll give him a buzz and see if he can come and stay. We won't be bored then. He'll have us screaming in terror every minute we're awake, he will.'

'I'm not sure that's such a good idea,' said Wally.

'Oh, please, Wally boy,' said Foulpest. 'I've got to have a proper perishing scare soon or I'll go potty.'

'Anyway, I thought Mummies were Egyptian,' said Wally, 'and called things like Tutankhamun and Rama-something-or-other. Eamonn doesn't sound like a very Egyptian name to me.'

'No,' said Foulpest, 'his real name's Amenhotep, but I can't say that, so I just calls him Eamonn.'

'But you just did say it,' said Wally.

'What?' said Foulpest.

'"Amenhotep",' said Wally.

'Who's that?' said Foulpest.

'Your friend Eamonn,' said Wally, 'he's Amenhotep. That's his real name.'

'"Amenhotep"?' said Foulpest. 'Yes, but I can't say that. It's far too complicated. That's why I just calls him Eamonn.'

That sounded so bonkers Wally's brain felt like it was going to split in half.

'But you just DID say "Amenho—"' Wally began.

'Oh, we're never going to find this perishing bucket,' said Foulpest. 'Just let me get a jumper from my room and then we'll go down and have a drink and a biscuit and see what's on television.'

'But what about the bucket of brunge?' asked Wally.

'Don't worry, Wally,' said Foulpest. 'It's bound to turn up sooner or later.' Before Wally could say any more, Foulpest pushed open his bedroom door and went in.

'Argh!' cried Foulpest.

'Uncle Foulpest?' said Wally, running in after him.

Foulpest was stomping around the room, covered in horrible-looking brown stuff.

He had found the door with the missing bucket of brunge balanced on it.

'Ha ha ha!' chuckled Foulpest, spraying Wally with brunge. 'That was wonderful!'

'Isn't it wonderful, children?' said Miss Keen the teacher next Monday in class. 'This Friday, we're all going on a school trip!'

'Brilliant!' said Tommy.

'Wicked!' said Sam.

'Boring!' said Bernard.

'Bernard!' said Miss Keen. 'I'll be sending

a letter home telling you all about it,' she went on, 'and we'll have a few spare seats on the coach so if any of your parents or carers want to come along, they'd be most welcome.'

'Oh dear,' thought Wally. Foulpest would want to come along all right. He was still bored, despite the fun he'd had when the bucket of brunge had fallen on him.

'I suppose it would be better than having his friend Eamonn come to visit,' Wally thought.

But would it?

Wally remembered what happened when Foulpest came along to his parents' evening. And on the school trip to the art gallery. And the zoo. And the museum.

Oh, the museum! Wally went cold all over just thinking about it.

Perhaps he could lose the letter. Or feed it to the school guinea-pig.

No. Wally was a good boy. He couldn't do that to a proper school letter.

He could ask Mrs Beamish, the nice old lady from next door, if she'd like to come along instead. Mrs Beamish was friendly, kind and helpful, and baked really wonderful fairy cakes. *She* wouldn't sit on thousand-year-old pots and ruin them. *She* wouldn't draw funny moustaches and googly eyes on expensive paintings.

Not like certain people he could mention.

But he knew what Mrs Beamish would say. She would say that he had to ask Foulpest because, although Foulpest could be a bit clumsy, he had a good heart and a kind mind and didn't mean any harm.

Maybe he should just try not to worry. Maybe they'd be going somewhere Foulpest wouldn't be interested in, like a car park or a turnip farm or a factory that made cardigans or something.

Wally looked at the letter.

'Prepare for a scare and a spook and a fright!' it said. 'On Friday, we will be going on a school trip to Nervous Manor, the famous Haunted House!'

'A Haunted House?' thought Wally.

'I do hope your uncle will want to come along, Wally,' said Miss Keen. 'It's always good to see him.'

'Oh, he'll want to come along all right,' said Wally. 'Don't you worry.'

Wally's friends were delighted to see Foulpest on the day of the trip. They loved the idea of going to a haunted house with a real live ogre.

'Will you scare all the ghosts?' asked Tommy.

'I did scare a ghost once,' said Foulpest. 'He went as white as a sheet!'

Tommy and Sam and all the other children laughed.

Wally looked at his watch.

'We're going to be late,' he said.

'Have you been to lots of haunted houses?' asked Sam.

'Oh yes!' roared Foulpest. 'But there's something LOADS scarier than a haunted house - and that's a haunted toilet! Ooh, you don't know what frightened *is* until you've heard the ghastly gurgling of the freezing flush of fear!'

Again, the children laughed.

'When's that coach going to get here?' wondered Wally.

'Going by coach, are we?' said Foulpest. 'A big black coach, I'll be bound, driven by a headless coachman and pulled by four midnight horses with eyes as red as volcano sweets.'

'Volcano sweets?' said Sam.

'Blazing red and hard they is!' grinned Foulpest. 'And what a treat! You takes fistfuls of wasp juice and throws them in your nearest volcano till they set, then you eats as many of them as you can before your tongue falls out!'

'Here's the coach now,' said Miss Keen.

'Thank goodness!' said Wally.

The coach was disappointingly normal. It had wheels and an engine and went "hiss!" when it stopped.

As he climbed on board, Foulpest gave the driver a hard stare.

'That's never a proper head on top of his neck,' he said to Wally. 'It's just a plastic one he wears so people won't notice he's really a headless coachman! Let me give it one little twist and I'll prove it!'

Foulpest reached out to grab the driver's ears.

'No!' said Wally sharply and he quickly steered his uncle right to the very back of the coach.

Maybe if they sat miles away from everyone else and kept quiet, Foulpest wouldn't embarrass him any more.

Fat chance.

No sooner had Foulpest and Wally sat

down, than Bernard plonked himself on the seat next to them.

He was cramming handfuls of chocolate and sweets and crisps into his mouth all at once. Plenty were getting lost on the way, though, and he was covered in crumbs and melted toffee and chocolate stains.

'Dried off, then, have you?' Bernard said to Wally with a horrible smile, but his mouth was so full it sounded more like 'Fwide fwoff wenn, habb woo?'

Wally ignored him and hoped Bernard would lose interest.

No such luck.

'I want to be scared at this haunted house,' said Bernard. 'But it better be a proper scare or I'll thump someone.'

'Yeah, I could do with a proper scare

too,' said Foulpest.

Bernard stared at Foulpest.

'You all right, boy?' Foulpest said in a friendly voice and he smiled at Bernard, showing all his broken brown teeth.

Bernard blinked.

'Hey,' said Bernard, pointing at Foulpest. 'I've never looked at him properly before,

Wally, but your uncle is really, really ugly.'

Now, calling an ogre 'ugly' is the greatest compliment you can pay him, and Foulpest was delighted.

'Thank you, boy,' he said, smiling even more widely so that Bernard could see the mould growing on his gums. 'That's a lovely thing to say!'

Bernard didn't understand why Foulpest wasn't annoyed at his rudeness. He would have to try harder.

'And you've got great big pointy ears with hair sticking out of them!' he said.

'I know,' said Foulpest. 'Horrible, ain't they? See how the crumbs of earwax sparkle as they cling to the hairs.'

'And broken brown teeth,' said Bernard.

'I have,' said Foulpest proudly, 'and all of them me own!'

'And warts!'

'Them's just the few that you can see. Take a look at this!'

Before Wally could stop him, Foulpest had rolled his sock down and was showing Bernard his favourite crop of warts.

Wally knew that Bernard enjoyed

being the most revolting person around, and that Bernard would want to get his own back on Foulpest. So he wasn't surprised when Bernard flopped down onto the floor and slipped the joke spider onto his tummy. Bernard cried out, 'It's jumped on me! A great big poisonous spider has—'

But before Bernard could finish – and before Wally could point out that it wasn't a real great big poisonous spider – Foulpest had grabbed the spider and popped it in his mouth.

'Don't worry, boy,' he said to Bernard, 'great big poisonous spiders are one of my favourite snacks!

Ooh, mind you, though,' Foulpest went on, 'this one's a bit rubbery, isn't it?'

But Bernard wasn't finished yet. Wally could see that he was still eager to prove he could be more disgusting than Foulpest.

'Right,' said Bernard. He stuck his finger as far up his nose as it would go and pulled out an enormous bogey. 'Look at this!' he said, brandishing the bogey at Foulpest.

'What do you call that?' said Foulpest.

'I call that a bogey!' said Bernard.

'*That's* not a bogey, lad,' said Foulpest. He put a fingernail into his nostril and scooped out something that was as large and green and crinkly as a crocodile's head. 'Now *that's* a bogey!'

Bernard took one look at Foulpest's bogey and went grey. Without another word, he ran to the front of the coach to find Miss Keen.

'Poor little chap,' said Foulpest. 'He must be travel-sick.'

Wally just shook his head.

§Ο─Φ─Ο─ε

Shortly afterwards, they arrived at Nervous Manor. It was a spiky, spooky haunted house.

On the huge black

front doors was a sign that read,

Abandon hope all ye who enter here!

and, underneath it, another that read,

No milk on Wednesdays, thank you.

Before Miss Keen could reach up to ring the bell, the doors swung open.

'Gulp!' said Sam, and he took hold of Miss Keen's hand.

'Well, I suppose we should go in,' said Miss Keen.

'Yeah, come on, let's get on with it,' said Bernard, pushing past her and into the house. He was feeling better now he'd eaten a whole packet of chocolate biscuits. 'Well, what are you waiting for?' he called out once he was inside. 'I'm looking for a proper scare.'

'Quite right too, lad,' said Foulpest, and

everyone followed Bernard inside.

Foulpest took a deep breath and looked around.

'It's gloomy, it's cold and it stinks,' he said with a happy smile. 'I often wonder why your Mum and Dad don't get themselves a nice cosy place like this, Wally.'

Before Wally could reply, the guide appeared. He was a little man with a pointy nose.

And he was running for his life down the stairs.

'Ghosts!' he cried. 'Goblins! Ghoulies! Heeeelp!'

A ghost came charging down after him, clanking its chains.

'Woooooaaaaaahhhhh!' it wailed in a ghostly voice.

'That's spooky!' cried Miss Keen.

'That's scary!' cried Sam.

'That's rubbish!' said Bernard. 'It's not a real ghost! Look, it's wearing sandals.'

Bernard put his foot out. The ghost tripped over and fell into a suit of armour.

'Oww!' said the ghost, in a not very ghostly voice. It limped off up the stairs again.

'It's a good job you're here, sonny,' said the little man with the pointy nose, 'thanks for saving me.' But he didn't sound like he meant it.

'I'm looking for a proper scare,' said Bernard. 'And if I don't get one, I'm going to thump someone.'

'Good luck,' said the little man. 'Now, ladies and gentlemen, boys and girls, I bid you welcome to Nervous Manor – the most haunted Haunted House in England. My name is Gordon, and I will be your guide today on our Tour of Terror!'

'Tour of rubbish, more like,' said Bernard.

Miss Keen gave him a stern look, and Bernard shut up.

Eek-eek! Eek-eek!

'What is that terrible creaky squeaking?' said Gordon as they climbed the stairs of the haunted house.

'It sounds like your bottom,' said Bernard.

'Bernard!' snapped Miss Keen.

'It's coming from that room over there,' said Wally.

'I do believe you're right, young man,' said Gordon. 'Are we feeling brave?'

'Um,' said Sam uncertainly.

'Always!' said Tommy.

'Shall we investigate?' said Gordon.

'Yes!' said Tommy.

'I suppose,' said Sam, taking care to hold on tight to Miss Keen's hand.

'Yawn,' said Bernard. 'I'm hungry.'

Wally wasn't scared – of course he wasn't – but all the same he was very pleased that Foulpest was next to him as they followed the sound of squeaking to a large bedroom.

The squeaking was coming from a rocking chair in the corner.

A lady in an old-fashioned dress was sitting in it, rocking backwards and forwards!

Eek-eek! Eek-eek!

'Oh my word!' said Gordon. 'It's the Rocking Chair Lady!'

'The Rocking Chair Lady?' said Sam anxiously. He decided now would be a good time to stand behind Miss Keen.

'The Rocking Chair Lady has sat in that chair for a hundred years now,' Gordon went on. 'If anyone is foolish enough to go near her, she grabs them by the hands and . . . rocks them to death!'

Sam put his hands in his pockets.

'She's a very ugly woman,' said Bernard.

'Ah,' said Foulpest. 'He's such a perishing polite little boy, isn't he?'

'In fact,' said Bernard, 'she looks like a man.'

'Be quiet, Bernard,' said Wally. 'You're spoiling it!'

'And she's wearing the same sandals as that ghost,' said Bernard. 'I'm going to have a closer look.'

'Don't go near her, sonny,' said Gordon.

'I'll give her a rocking all right,' said Bernard.

'Do as you're told, Bernard,' said Miss Keen.

Wally had had enough of Bernard's showing off. He reached out to stop him, but Bernard slipped past.

'Rock-a-bye Lady, on the treetop. . .' Bernard sang as he shook the rocking chair as hard as he could.

'Oi, geddoff, sonny!' said the Rocking Chair Lady in a man's voice.

'And down will come Lady, rocker and all!' sang Bernard.

'Argh!' said the Rocking Chair Lady as she went flying out of her chair and into the fireplace.

'Ha ha! She's off her rocker!' laughed Bernard. 'I told you this was rubbish. I want a proper scare!'

'Bernard,' said Miss Keen, 'come here at once!'

'Ooh, my head!' moaned The Rocking Chair Lady from the fireplace.

'Perhaps we'd better stop for lunch now,' said Gordon. 'I think Colin – er, I mean the Rocking Chair Lady – needs an ambulance.'

'I hope you're proud of yourself!' said Wally. 'You ruined the whole morning!'

The children were sitting in the cafeteria, having their packed lunches. Miss Keen had gone off to make sure the Rocking

Chair Lady was all right and Foulpest had also disappeared, but Wally was too cross with Bernard to wonder where.

'There's no need to thank me!' laughed Bernard. 'Just give me your packed lunch.'

'No,' said Wally. 'Don't be so rude!'

'Give it!' said Bernard.

'Eat your own!' said Wally.

'I already have,' said Bernard. 'I'm still hungry.'

'Serves you right for being so greedy!' said Wally.

'I'll pour orange drink all over it!' said Bernard.

'If you've already had your lunch, you don't have any orange drink left,' said Wally.

Bernard didn't have a good answer to this, so he just grabbed Wally's lunchbox.

Wally grabbed
it back.

Bernard
pulled.

Wally pulled.

They both went
red in the face.

'Let go!' said Wally.

'Or you'll what?' said
Bernard. 'You haven't got that
big fat ugly ogre to protect you now!'

'Don't you talk about my uncle like
that!' said Wally.

'Where's he gone anyway?' said
Bernard. 'I bet he's off picking his warts
and eating the grot from under his
toenails!'

Wally thought he probably was but

he didn't say anything.

'Wally's uncle is a fatso!' chanted Bernard.

'Shut up!' said Wally.

'Wally's uncle's a fatsooo!' Bernard continued.

'My uncle made this packed lunch!' said Wally.

Then he thought to himself, 'My uncle made this packed lunch.'

And that gave him an idea.

Wally let go of the lunchbox.

'Argh!' cried Bernard as he went stumbling across the haunted house dining room and banged into the wall.

Wally laughed.

'I don't know what you're laughing about!' said Bernard crossly. 'I've got your packed lunch that your fatso ogre uncle made! And I'm going to eat it in front of you!'

Bernard opened the lunchbox.

'What have we got here?' he said. 'Oh, scrummy sandwiches! Yum!'

He took one out and crammed it into his mouth.

'Tasty!' Bernard said with his mouth full. 'I bet you wish you were eating this, it's all delicious and crunchy. What's in it? Peanut butter?'

'Dung beetles,' said Wally. He'd told him not to, but Foulpest kept giving him dung beetle sandwiches. He said the shells were good for your teeth and the dung put hairs on your chest.

'Liar!' said Bernard. But he spat the sandwich out, just in case. 'Anyway, never mind that, I'm having some of these crisps too! What flavour are they?'

'Cheese and bunion,' said Wally.

'They are not!' said Bernard, mashing a handful of them into his mouth and chewing. 'Oh dear! Are they?'

'That's why they're so green and crackly,' said Wally.

'Bleurgh!' said Bernard. He went grey again. 'Water!'

'I wouldn't drink that if I were you,' said Wally.

But it was too late. Bernard had taken the drink out of the lunchbox and was gulping it down.

He'd had more than half of it before Wally had a chance to say, 'It's slime juice cordial with whizzed-up vampire bats in it. Can't you taste the fangs?'

Bernard spent the next half hour in the toilet.

'Poor little soldier,' said Foulpest when he heard about Bernard.

'I don't know about that, Uncle,' said Wally. 'He's behaved very badly.'

'You shouldn't be so hard on the lad,' said Foulpest. 'He's just disappointed he ain't had no proper scare yet.'

'Anyway, what have you been up to?' said Wally.

'Well, it's funny you should ask,' said Foulpest. 'Remember how I was telling you that I was getting bored because I ain't had no proper scare either...'

He was going to say more when Miss Keen clapped her hands for silence.

'Now, children,' said Miss Keen, 'Clear away your lunch things, please. Gordon tells me that we can go on with our tour of the house.'

'Welcome to the Egyptian room,' said Gordon. 'The owners of Nervous Manor were very interested in ancient Egypt. All the statues and coffins you see around you were brought back by the great explorer, Sir Alexander Nervous. Sir Alexander was on the dig that uncovered the tomb of the Pharaoh Rammallammadingdong the Second. But beware! For in opening the tomb, Sir Alexander brought down upon himself and this house the terrible. . . Curse of the Mummy!'

'Not the sort of mummy who has babies! Hor hor hor!' chortled Foulpest. He still thought that was the funniest thing he'd ever heard.

'The curse of your mum's bum, more like!' said Bernard.

'Shush!' said Wally.

'Never you mind "Shush!", Wally,' said Bernard. He was feeling better now he'd eaten two bumper bags of toffees. 'I'm going to get you for that.'

'Get me for what?' said Wally.

'Tricking me into eating your disgusting packed lunch!'

'I didn't trick you,' said Wally, 'you stole it!'

'Did not!'

'Did too!'

'Did not!'

'Did too!'

'Wally, Bernard - behave, please!' said Miss Keen.

Just then, one of the coffins began to rattle.

'Look out, children, it's the Mummy!' said Gordon. 'He's rising from the grave!'

'Oh brilliant!' said Tommy.

'Oh dear,' said Sam.

'Oh boring,' said Bernard.

'Bernard!' said Miss Keen.

Creeeeaaaaakk!

The lid of the coffin slowly opened and out crawled. . .

The Mummy!

'Wooooooaaaaaaaaaahhh!' it wailed. 'I am the Mummy and I have come to frighten you into the middle of next week!'

It was wrapped in very old bandages and covered in cobwebs and it smelled horrible.

'I am looking for the boy called Bernard,' it said in a very creepy voice.

'You don't frighten me,' said Bernard.

'Where is the boy called Bernard?' said the Mummy.

'That's never a real Mummy!' said Bernard. 'It's the same man who played the ghost and the Rocking Chair Lady.

They must have bandaged him up in the ambulance.'

The Mummy put its arms out. It began walking towards Bernard.

'Give me the boy called Bernard,' it said.

'It's easy to tell because he wears sandals,' said Bernard.

'But the Mummy *isn't* wearing sandals,' said Wally. 'Look.'

Bernard looked. Wally was right. The Mummy

wasn't wearing sandals.

At that moment, the door opened. A man in a very bad Mummy outfit came in. He was wearing sandals.

'I told you not to start without me, Gordon,' said the man.

'Colin!' said Gordon. 'But I thought you were pretending to be the Mummy. If you've only just come in, who's that?'

And he pointed at the Mummy.

The Mummy was just about to grab Bernard.

'It must be. . .'

'A *real* Mummy!' chuckled Foulpest. 'Look how scary he is! Hor hor hor!'

'Argh!' screamed Bernard. He turned and fled.

'What's he running away for?' said Foulpest. 'I thought he wanted to have a proper scare.'

'I think he's changed his mind,' said Wally and he pointed at the Mummy who was chasing Bernard around Nervous Manor. 'That's your friend Eamonn, isn't it?'

'Yeah,' said Foulpest. 'He's terrifying, isn't he? Gives me the willies just watching him - and, oh, what a revolting pong!'

Bernard certainly thought so. He was holding his nose with both hands as he ran.

'Eamonn's such a lovely bloke,' said Foulpest. 'The moment I told him about this kid who wanted a proper scare, Eamonn said he had to meet him.'

'So *that's* what you were doing while we were having lunch,' said Wally. 'Getting you friend Eamonn to come here?'

'That's right,' said Foulpest. 'Well, I had to do something for the little chap after he was so sweet to me on the coach. Calling me "ugly" like that, and feeding me a poisonous spider and showing me his bogeys and everything.'

As Bernard ran past, he grabbed Wally.

'Help me, Wally! Please!' he cried.

'But you told me you never need help,'

said Wally. 'Not from me, anyway.'

'That was different!' said Bernard. 'Oh no! He's catching up!' and Bernard let go of Wally and ran off.

'He does look a bit tired, though,' said Foulpest.

'Bernard's not all that used to running,' said Wally.

'Should I tell Eamonn to stop?' said Foulpest.

'Mmm. . .' said Wally thoughtfully. 'Not just yet. We don't want to spoil Bernard's fun, do we?'

'I'll get you for this, Wally!' cried Bernard. 'I'll put a cactus in your swimming trunks and scorpions in your school dinners and. . . and. . . Ooh dear!'

'Did you hear that?' said Foulpest.
'What a lovely lad!'

'Mmm,' said Wally. 'Lovely.'

And Foulpest and Wally both smiled.

THE END